VALLEY OF DREAMS

VALLEY OF DREAMS

by Stanley G. Weinbaum

Captain Harrison of the *Ares* expedition turned away from the little telescope in the bow of the rocket. "Two weeks more, at the most," he remarked. "Mars only retrogrades for seventy days in all, relative to the earth, and we've got to be homeward bound during that period, or wait a year and a half for old Mother Earth to go around the sun and catch up with us again. How'd you like to spend a winter here?"

Dick Jarvis, chemist of the party, shivered as he looked up from his notebook. "I'd just as soon spend it in a liquid air tank!" he averred. "These eighty-below zero summer nights are plenty for me."

"Well," mused the captain, "the first successful Martian expedition ought to be home long before then."

"Successful if we get home," corrected Jarvis. "I don't trust these cranky rockets—not since the auxiliary dumped me in the middle of Thyle last week. Walking back from a rocket ride is a new sensation to me."

"Which reminds me," returned Harrison, "that we've got to recover your films. They're important if we're to pull this trip out of the red. Remember how the public mobbed the first moon pictures? Our shots ought to pack 'em to the doors. And the broadcast rights, too; we might show a profit for the Academy."

"What interests me," countered Jarvis, "is a personal profit. A book, for instance; exploration books are always popular. *Martian Deserts*—how's that for a title?"

"Lousy!" grunted the captain. "Sounds like a cook-book for desserts. You'd have to call it 'Love Life of a Martian,' or something like that."

Jarvis chuckled. "Anyway," he said, "if we once get back home, I'm going to grab what profit there is, and never, never, get any farther from the earth than a good stratosphere plane'll take me. I've learned to appreciate the planet after plowing over this dried-up pill we're on

5

now."

"I'll lay you odds you'll be back here year after next," grinned the Captain. "You'll want to visit your pal—that trick ostrich."

"Tweel?" The other's tone sobered. "I wish I hadn't lost him, at that. He was a good scout. I'd never have survived the dream-beast but for him. And that battle with the push-cart things—I never even had a chance to thank him."

"A pair of lunatics, you two," observed Harrison. He squinted through the port at the gray gloom of the Mare Cimmerium. "There comes the sun." He paused. "Listen, Dick—you and Leroy take the other auxiliary rocket and go out and salvage those films."

Jarvis stared. "Me and Leroy?" he echoed ungrammatically. "Why not me and Putz? An engineer would have some chance of getting us there and back if the rocket goes bad on us."

The captain nodded toward the stern, whence issued at that moment a medley of blows and guttural expletives. "Putz is going over the insides of the Ares," he announced. "He'll have his hands full until we leave, because I want every bolt inspected. It's too late for repairs once we cast off."

"And if Leroy and I crack up? That's our last auxiliary."

"Pick up another ostrich and walk back," suggested Harrison gruffly. Then he smiled. "If you have trouble, we'll hunt you out in the Ares," he finished. "Those films are important." He turned. "Leroy!"

The dapper little biologist appeared, his face questioning.

"You and Jarvis are off to salvage the auxiliary," the Captain said. "Everything's ready and you'd better start now. Call back at half-hour intervals; I'll be listening."

Leroy's eyes glistened. "Perhaps we land for specimens—no?" he queried.

"Land if you want to. This golf ball seems safe enough."

"Except for the dream-beast," muttered Jarvis with a faint shudder. He frowned suddenly. "Say, as long as we're going that way, suppose I have a look for Tweel's home! He must live off there somewhere, and he's the most important thing we've seen on Mars."

Harrison hesitated. "If I thought you could keep out of trouble," he muttered. "All right," he decided. "Have a look. There's food and water aboard the auxiliary; you can take a couple of days. But keep in touch with me, you saps!"

Jarvis and Leroy went through the airlock out to the grey plain. The thin air, still scarcely warmed by the rising sun, bit flesh and lung like needles, and they gasped with a sense of suffocation. They dropped to a sitting posture, waiting for their bodies, trained by months in acclimatization chambers back on earth, to accommodate themselves to the tenuous air. Leroy's face, as always, turned a smothered blue, and Jarvis heard his own breath rasping and rattling in his throat. But in five minutes, the discomfort passed; they rose and entered the little auxiliary rocket that rested beside the black hull of the *Ares*.

The under-jets roared out their fiery atomic blast; dirt and bits of shattered biopods spun away in a cloud as the rocket rose. Harrison watched the projectile trail its flaming way into the south, then turned back to his work.

It was four days before he saw the rocket again. Just at evening, as the sun dropped behind the horizon with the suddenness of a candle falling into the sea, the auxiliary flashed out of the southern heavens, easing gently down on the flaming wings of the under-jets. Jarvis and Leroy emerged, passed through the swiftly gathering dusk, and faced him in the light of the *Ares*. He surveyed the two; Jarvis was tattered and scratched, but apparently in better condition than Leroy, whose dapperness was completely lost. The little biologist was pale as the nearer moon that glowed outside; one arm was bandaged in thermo-skin and his clothes hung in veritable rags. But it was his eyes that struck Harrison most strangely; to one who lived these many weary days with the diminutive Frenchman, there was something queer about them. They were frightened, plainly enough, and that was odd, since Leroy was no coward or he'd never have been one of the four chosen by the Academy for the first Martian expedition. But the fear in his eyes was more understandable than that other expression, that queer fixity of gaze like one in a trance, or like a person in an ecstasy. "Like a chap who's seen Heaven and Hell together," Harrison expressed it to himself. He was yet to discover how right he was.

He assumed a gruffness as the weary pair sat down. "You're a fine looking couple!" he growled. "I should've known better than to let you wander off alone." He paused. "Is your arm all right, Leroy? Need any treatment?"

Jarvis answered. "It's all right—just gashed. No danger of infection here, I guess; Leroy says there aren't any microbes on Mars."

"Well," exploded the Captain, "Let's hear it, then! Your radio reports sounded screwy. 'Escaped from Paradise!' Huh!"

"I didn't want to give details on the radio," said Jarvis soberly. "You'd have thought we'd gone loony."

"I think so, anyway."

"*Moi aussi!*" muttered Leroy. "I too!"

"Shall I begin at the beginning?" queried the chemist. "Our early reports were pretty nearly complete." He stared at Putz, who had come in silently, his face and hands blackened with carbon, and seated himself beside Harrison.

"At the beginning," the Captain decided.

"Well," began Jarvis, "we got started all right, and flew due south along the meridian of the *Ares*, same course I'd followed last week. I was getting used to this narrow horizon, so I didn't feel so much like being cooped under a big bowl, but one does keep overestimating distances. Something four miles away looks eight when you're used to terrestrial curvature, and that makes you guess its size just four times too large. A little hill looks like a mountain until you're almost over it."

"I know that," grunted Harrison.

"Yes, but Leroy didn't, and I spent our first couple of hours trying to explain it to him. By the time he understood (if he does yet) we were past Cimmerium and over that Xanthus desert, and then we crossed the canal with the mud city and the barrel-shaped citizens and the place where Tweel had shot the dream-beast. And nothing would do for Pierre here but that we put down so he could practice his biology on the remains. So we did.

"The thing was still there. No sign of decay; couldn't be, of course, without bacterial forms of life, and Leroy says that Mars is as sterile as an operating table."

"*Comme le coeur d'une fileuse,*" corrected the little biologist, who was beginning to regain a trace of his usual energy. "Like an old maid's heart!"

"However," resumed Jarvis, "about a hundred of the little grey-green biopods had fastened onto the thing and were growing and branching. Leroy found a stick and knocked 'em off, and each branch broke away and became a biopod crawling around with the others. So he poked around at the creature, while I looked away from it; even dead, that rope-armed devil gave me the creeps. And then came the surprise; the thing was part plant!"

"*C'est vrai!*" confirmed the biologist. "It's true!"

"It was a big cousin of the biopods," continued Jarvis. "Leroy was quite excited; he figures that all Martian life is of that sort—neither

9

plant nor animal. Life here never differentiated, he says; everything has both natures in it, even the barrel-creatures—even Tweel! I think he's right, especially when I recall how Tweel rested, sticking his beak in the ground and staying that way all night. I never saw him eat or drink, either; perhaps his beak was more in the nature of a root, and he got his nourishment that way."

"Sounds nutty to me," observed Harrison.

"Well," continued Jarvis, "we broke up a few of the other growths and they acted the same way—the pieces crawled around, only much slower than the biopods, and then stuck themselves in the ground. Then Leroy had to catch a sample of the walking grass, and we were ready to leave when a parade of the barrel-creatures rushed by with their push-carts. They hadn't forgotten me, either; they all drummed out, 'We are v-r-r-iends—ouch!' just as they had before. Leroy wanted to shoot one and cut it up, but I remembered the battle Tweel and I had had with them, and vetoed the idea. But he did hit on a possible explanation as to what they did with all the rubbish they gathered."

"Made mud-pies, I guess," grunted the captain.

"More or less," agreed Jarvis. "They use it for food, Leroy thinks. If they're part vegetable, you see, that's what they'd want—soil with organic remains in it to make it fertile. That's why they ground up sand and biopods and other growths all together. See?"

"Dimly," countered Harrison. "How about the suicides?"

"Leroy had a hunch there, too. The suicides jump into the grinder when the mixture has too much sand and gravel; they throw themselves in to adjust the proportions."

"Rats!" said Harrison disgustedly. "Why couldn't they bring in some extra branches from outside?"

"Because suicide is easier. You've got to remember that these creatures can't be judged by earthly standards; they probably don't feel pain, and they haven't got what we'd call individuality. Any intelligence they have is the property of the whole community—like an ant-heap. That's it! Ants are willing to die for their ant-hill; so are these creatures."

"So are men," observed the captain, "if it comes to that."

"Yes, but men aren't exactly eager. It takes some emotion like patriotism to work 'em to the point of dying for their country; these things do it all in the day's work." He paused.

"Well, we took some pictures of the dream-beast and the barrel-creatures, and then we started along. We sailed over Xanthus, keeping as close to the meridian of the *Ares* as we could, and pretty soon we crossed the trail of the pyramid-builder. So we circled back to let Leroy take a look at it, and when we found it, we landed. The thing had completed just two rows of bricks since Tweel and I left it, and there it was, breathing in silicon and breathing out bricks as if it had eternity to do it in—which it has. Leroy wanted to dissect it with a Boland explosive bullet, but I thought that anything that had lived for ten million years was entitled to the respect due old age, so I talked him out of it. He peeped into the hole on top of it and nearly got beaned by the arm coming up with a brick, and then he chipped off a few pieces of it, which didn't disturb the creature a bit. He found the place I'd chipped, tried to see if there was any sign of healing, and decided he could tell better in two or three thousand years. So we took a few shots of it and sailed on.

"Mid afternoon we located the wreck of my rocket. Not a thing disturbed; we picked up my films and tried to decide what next. I wanted to find Tweel if possible; I figured from the fact of his pointing south that he lived somewhere near Thyle. We plotted our route and judged that the desert we were in now was Thyle II; Thyle

I should be east of us. So, on a hunch, we decided to have a look at Thyle I, and away we buzzed."

"*Der* motors?" queried Putz, breaking his long silence.

"For a wonder, we had no trouble, Karl. Your blast worked perfectly. So we hummed along, pretty high to get a wider view, I'd say about fifty thousand feet. Thyle II spread out like an orange carpet, and after a while we came to the grey branch of the Mare Chronium that bounded it. That was narrow; we crossed it in half an hour, and there was Thyle I—same orange-hued desert as its mate. We veered south, toward the Mare Australe, and followed the edge of the desert. And toward sunset we spotted it."

"Shpotted?" echoed Putz. "Vot vas shpotted?"

"The desert was spotted—with buildings! Not one of the mud cities of the canals, although a canal went through it. From the map we figured the canal was a continuation of the one Schiaparelli called Ascanius.

"We were probably too high to be visible to any inhabitants of the city, but also too high for a good look at it, even with the glasses. However, it was nearly sunset, anyway, so we didn't plan on dropping in. We circled the place; the canal went out into the Mare Australe, and there, glittering in the south, was the melting polar ice-cap! The canal drained it; we could distinguish the sparkle of water in it. Off to the southeast, just at the edge of the Mare Australe, was a valley—the first irregularity I'd seen on Mars except the cliffs that bounded Xanthus and Thyle II. We flew over the valley—" Jarvis paused suddenly and shuddered; Leroy, whose color had begun to return, seemed to pale. The chemist resumed, "Well, the valley looked all right—then! Just a gray waste, probably full of crawlers like the others.

"We circled back over the city; say, I want to tell you that place was—well, gigantic! It was colossal; at first I thought the size was due to that illusion I spoke of—you know, the nearness of the horizon—but it wasn't that. We sailed right over it, and you've never seen anything like it!

"But the sun dropped out of sight right then. I knew we were pretty far south—latitude 60—but I didn't know just how much night we'd have."

Harrison glanced at a Schiaparelli chart. "About 60—eh?" he said. "Close to what corresponds to the Antarctic circle. You'd have about four hours of night at this season. Three months from now you'd have none at all."

"Three months!" echoed Jarvis, surprised. Then he grinned. "Right! I forget the seasons here are twice as long as ours. Well, we sailed out into the desert about twenty miles, which put the city below the horizon in case we overslept, and there we spent the night.

"You're right about the length of it. We had about four hours of darkness which left us fairly rested. We ate breakfast, called our location to you, and started over to have a look at the city.

"We sailed toward it from the east and it loomed up ahead of us like a range of mountains. Lord, what a city! Not that New York mightn't have higher buildings, or Chicago cover more ground, but for sheer mass, those structures were in a class by themselves. Gargantuan!

"There was a queer look about the place, though. You know how a terrestrial city sprawls out, a nimbus of suburbs, a ring of residential sections, factory districts, parks, highways. There was none of that here; the city rose out of the desert as abruptly as a cliff. Only a few little sand mounds marked the division, and then the walls of those gigantic structures.

"The architecture was strange, too. There were lots of devices that are impossible back home, such as set-backs in reverse, so that a building with a small base could spread out as it rose. That would be a valuable trick in New York, where land is almost priceless, but to do it, you'd have to transfer Martian gravitation there!

"Well, since you can't very well land a rocket in a city street, we put down right next to the canal side of the city, took our small cameras and revolvers, and started for a gap in the wall of masonry. We weren't ten feet from the rocket when we both saw the explanation for a lot of the queerness.

"The city was in ruin! Abandoned, deserted, dead as Babylon! Or at least, so it looked to us then, with its empty streets which, if they had been paved, were now deep under sand."

"A ruin, eh?" commented Harrison. "How old?"

"How could we tell?" countered Jarvis. "The next expedition to this golf ball ought to carry an archeologist—and a philologist, too, as we found out later. But it's a devil of a job to estimate the age of anything here; things weather so slowly that most of the buildings might have been put up yesterday. No rainfall, no earthquakes, no vegetation is here to spread cracks with its roots—nothing. The only aging factors here are the erosion of the wind—and that's negligible in this atmosphere—and the cracks caused by changing temperature. And one other agent—meteorites. They must crash down occasionally on the city, judging from the thinness of the air, and the fact that we've seen four strike ground right here near the *Ares*."

"Seven," corrected the captain. "Three dropped while you were gone."

"Well, damage by meteorites must be slow, anyway. Big ones would be as rare here as on earth, because big ones get through in spite of the atmosphere, and those buildings could sustain a lot of little ones.

My guess at the city's age—and it may be wrong by a big percentage—would be fifteen thousand years. Even that's thousands of years older than any human civilization; fifteen thousand years ago was the Late Stone Age in the history of mankind.

"So Leroy and I crept up to those tremendous buildings feeling like pygmies, sort of awe-struck, and talking in whispers. I tell you, it was ghostly walking down that dead and deserted street, and every time we passed through a shadow, we shivered, and not just because shadows are cold on Mars. We felt like intruders, as if the great race that had built the place might resent our presence even across a hundred and fifty centuries. The place was as quiet as a grave, but we kept imagining things and peeping down the dark lanes between buildings and looking over our shoulders. Most of the structures were windowless, but when we did see an opening in those vast walls, we couldn't look away, expecting to see some horror peering out of it.

"Then we passed an edifice with an open arch; the doors were there, but blocked open by sand. I got up nerve enough to take a look inside, and then, of course, we discovered we'd forgotten to take our flashes. But we eased a few feet into the darkness and the passage debouched into a colossal hall. Far above us a little crack let in a pallid ray of daylight, not nearly enough to light the place; I couldn't even see if the hall rose clear to the distant roof. But I know the place was enormous; I said something to Leroy and a million thin echoes came slipping back to us out of the darkness. And after that, we began to hear other sounds—slithering rustling noises, and whispers, and sounds like suppressed breathing—and something black and silent passed between us and that far-away crevice of light.

"Then we saw three little greenish spots of luminosity in the dusk to our left. We stood staring at them, and suddenly they all shifted at once. Leroy yelled '*Ce sont des yeux!*' and they were! They were eyes!

15

VALLEY OF DREAMS

"Well, we stood frozen for a moment, while Leroy's yell reverberated back and forth between the distant walls, and the echoes repeated the words in queer, thin voices. There were mumblings and mutterings and whisperings and sounds like strange soft laughter, and then the three-eyed thing moved again. Then we broke for the door!

"We felt better out in the sunlight; we looked at each other sheepishly, but neither of us suggested another look at the buildings inside—though we *did* see the place later, and that was queer, too—but you'll hear about it when I come to it. We just loosened our revolvers and crept on along that ghostly street.

"The street curved and twisted and subdivided. I kept careful note of our directions, since we couldn't risk getting lost in that gigantic maze. Without our thermo-skin bags, night would finish us, even if what lurked in the ruins didn't. By and by, I noticed that we were veering back toward the canal, the buildings ended and there were only a few dozen ragged stone huts which looked as though they might have been built of debris from the city. I was just beginning to feel a bit disappointed at finding no trace of Tweel's people here when we rounded a corner and there he was!

"I yelled 'Tweel!' but he just stared, and then I realized that he wasn't Tweel, but another Martian of his sort. Tweel's feathery appendages were more orange hued and he stood several inches taller than this one. Leroy was sputtering in excitement, and the Martian kept his vicious beak directed at us, so I stepped forward as peacemaker. I said 'Tweel?' very questioningly, but there was no result. I tried it a dozen times, and we finally had to give it up; we couldn't connect.

"Leroy and I walked toward the huts, and the Martian followed us. Twice he was joined by others, and each time I tried yelling 'Tweel'

16

at them but they just stared at us. So we ambled on with the three trailing us, and then it suddenly occurred to me that my Martian accent might be at fault. I faced the group and tried trilling it out the way Tweel himself did: 'T-r-r-rwee-r-rl!' Like that.

"And that worked! One of them spun his head around a full ninety degrees, and screeched 'T-r-r-rweee-r-rl!' and a moment later, like an arrow from a bow, Tweel came sailing over the nearer huts to land on his beak in front of me!

"Man, we were glad to see each other! Tweel set up a twittering and chirping like a farm in summer and went sailing up and coming down on his beak, and I would have grabbed his hands, only he wouldn't keep still long enough.

"The other Martians and Leroy just stared, and after a while, Tweel stopped bouncing, and there we were. We couldn't talk to each other any more than we could before, so after I'd said 'Tweel' a couple of times and he'd said 'Tick,' we were more or less helpless. However, it was only mid-morning, and it seemed important to learn all we could about Tweel and the city, so I suggested that he guide us around the place if he weren't busy. I put over the idea by pointing back at the buildings and then at him and us.

"Well, apparently he wasn't too busy, for he set off with us, leading the way with one of his hundred and fifty-foot nosedives that set Leroy gasping. When we caught up, he said something like 'one, one, two—two, two, four—no, no—yes, yes—rock—no breet!' That didn't seem to mean anything; perhaps he was just letting Leroy know that he could speak English, or perhaps he was merely running over his vocabulary to refresh his memory.

"Anyway, he showed us around. He had a light of sorts in his black pouch, good enough for small rooms, but simply lost in some of the colossal caverns we went through. Nine out of ten buildings meant absolutely nothing to us—just vast empty chambers, full of shadows and rustlings and echoes. I couldn't imagine their use; they didn't seem suitable for living quarters, or even for commercial purposes—trade and so forth; they might have been all right as power-houses, but what could have been the purpose of a whole city full? And where were the remains of the machinery?

"The place was a mystery. Sometimes Tweel would show us through a hall that would have housed an ocean-liner, and he'd seem to swell with pride—and we couldn't make a damn thing of it! As a display of architectural power, the city was colossal; as anything else it was just nutty!

"But we did see one thing that registered. We came to that same building Leroy and I had entered earlier—the one with the three eyes in it. Well, we were a little shaky about going in there, but Tweel twittered and trilled and kept saying, 'Yes, yes, yes!' so we followed him, staring nervously about for the thing that had watched us. However, that hall was just like the others, full of murmurs and slithering noises and shadowy things slipping away into corners. If the three-eyed creature were still there, it must have slunk away with the others.

"Tweel led us along the wall; his light showed a series of little alcoves, and in the first of these we ran into a puzzling thing—a very weird thing. As the light flashed into the alcove, I saw first just an empty space, and then, squatting on the floor, I saw—it! A little creature about as big as a large rat, it was, gray and huddled and evidently startled by our appearance. It had the queerest, most devilish little face!—pointed ears or horns and satanic eyes that seemed to sparkle with a sort of fiendish intelligence.

"Tweel saw it, too, and let out a screech of anger, and the creature rose on two pencil-thin legs and scuttled off with a half-terrified, half defiant squeak. It darted past us into the darkness too quickly even for Tweel, and as it ran, something waved on its body like the fluttering of a cape. Tweel screeched angrily at it and set up a shrill hullabaloo that sounded like genuine rage.

"But the thing was gone, and then I noticed the weirdest of imaginable details. Where it had squatted on the floor was—a book! It had been hunched over a book!

"I took a step forward; sure enough, there was some sort of inscription on the pages—wavy white lines like a seismograph record on black sheets like the material of Tweel's pouch. Tweel fumed and whistled in wrath, picked up the volume and slammed it into place on a shelf full of others. Leroy and I stared dumbfounded at each other.

"Had the little thing with the fiendish face been reading? Or was it simply eating the pages, getting physical nourishment rather than mental? Or had the whole thing been accidental?

"If the creature were some rat-like pest that destroyed books, Tweel's rage was understandable, but why should he try to prevent an intelligent being, even though of an alien race, from *reading*—if it *was* reading? I don't know; I did notice that the book was entirely undamaged, nor did I see a damaged book among any that we handled. But I have an odd hunch that if we knew the secret of the little cape-clothed imp, we'd know the mystery of the vast abandoned city and of the decay of Martian culture.

"Well, Tweel quieted down after a while and led us completely around that tremendous hall. It had been a library, I think; at least, there were thousands upon thousands of those queer black-paged volumes printed in wavy lines of white. There were pictures, too, in some; and some of these showed Tweel's people. That's a point, of course; it indicated that his race built the city and printed the books.

VALLEY OF DREAMS

I don't think the greatest philologist on earth will ever translate one line of those records; they were made by minds too different from ours.

"Tweel could read them, naturally. He twittered off a few lines, and then I took a few of the books, with his permission; he said 'no, no!' to some and 'yes, yes!' to others. Perhaps he kept back the ones his people needed, or perhaps he let me take the ones he thought we'd understand most easily. I don't know; the books are outside there in the rocket.

"Then he held that dim torch of his toward the walls, and they were pictured. Lord, what pictures! They stretched up and up into the blackness of the roof, mysterious and gigantic. I couldn't make much of the first wall; it seemed to be a portrayal of a great assembly of Tweel's people. Perhaps it was meant to symbolize Society or Government. But the next wall was more obvious; it showed creatures at work on a colossal machine of some sort, and that would be Industry or Science. The back wall had corroded away in part, from what we could see, I suspected the scene was meant to portray Art, but it was on the fourth wall that we got a shock that nearly dazed us.

"I think the symbol was Exploration or Discovery. This wall was a little plainer, because the moving beam of daylight from that crack lit up the higher surface and Tweel's torch illuminated the lower. We made out a giant seated figure, one of the beaked Martians like Tweel, but with every limb suggesting heaviness, weariness. The arms dropped inertly on the chair, the thin neck bent and the beak rested on the body, as if the creature could scarcely bear its own weight. And before it was a queer kneeling figure, and at sight of it, Leroy and I almost reeled against each other. It was, apparently, a man!"

"A man!" bellowed Harrison. "A man you say?"

"I said apparently," retorted Jarvis. "The artist had exaggerated the nose almost to the length of Tweel's beak, but the figure had black shoulder-length hair, and instead of the Martian four, there were *five* fingers on its outstretched hand! It was kneeling as if in worship of the Martian, and on the ground was what looked like a pottery bowl full of some food as an offering. Well! Leroy and I thought we'd gone screwy!"

"And Putz and I think so, too!" roared the captain.

"Maybe we all have," replied Jarvis, with a faint grin at the pale face of the little Frenchman, who returned it in silence. "Anyway," he continued, "Tweel was squeaking and pointing at the figure, and saying 'Tick! Tick!' so he recognized the resemblance—and never mind any cracks about my nose!" he warned the captain. "It was Leroy who made the important comment; he looked at the Martian and said 'Thoth! The god Thoth!'"

"*Oui!*" confirmed the biologist. "*Comme l'Egypte!*"

"Yeah," said Jarvis. "Like the Egyptian ibis-headed god—the one with the beak. Well, no sooner did Tweel hear the name Thoth than he set up a clamor of twittering and squeaking. He pointed at himself and said 'Thoth! Thoth!' and then waved his arm all around and repeated it. Of course he often did queer things, but we both thought we understood what he meant. He was trying to tell us that his race called themselves Thoth. Do you see what I'm getting at?"

"I see, all right," said Harrison. "You think the Martians paid a visit to the earth, and the Egyptians remembered it in their mythology. Well, you're off, then; there wasn't any Egyptian civilization fifteen thousand years ago."

"Wrong!" grinned Jarvis. "It's too bad we *haven't* an archeologist with us, but Leroy tells me that there was a stone-age culture in Egypt then, the pre-dynastic civilization."

"Well, even so, what of it?"

"Plenty! Everything in that picture proves my point. The attitude of the Martian, heavy and weary—that's the unnatural strain of terrestrial gravitation. The name Thoth; Leroy tells me Thoth was the Egyptian god of philosophy and the inventor of *writing*! Get that? They must have picked up the idea from watching the Martian take notes. It's too much for coincidence that Thoth should be beaked and ibis-headed, and that the beaked Martians call themselves Thoth."

"Well, I'll be hanged! But what about the nose on the Egyptian? Do you mean to tell me that stone-age Egyptians had longer noses than ordinary men?"

"Of course not! It's just that the Martians very naturally cast their paintings in Martianized form. Don't human beings tend to relate everything to themselves? That's why dugongs and manatees started the mermaid myths—sailors thought they saw human features on the beasts. So the Martian artist, drawing either from descriptions or imperfect photographs, naturally exaggerated the size of the human nose to a degree that looked normal to him. Or anyway, that's my theory."

"Well, it'll do as a theory," grunted Harrison. "What I want to hear is why you two got back here looking like a couple of year-before-last bird's nests."

Jarvis shuddered again, and cast another glance at Leroy. The little biologist was recovering some of his accustomed poise, but he returned the glance with an echo of the chemist's shudder.

"We'll get to that," resumed the latter. "Meanwhile I'll stick to Tweel and his people. We spent the better part of three days with them, as you know. I can't give every detail, but I'll summarize the important facts and give our conclusions, which may not be worth an inflated franc. It's hard to judge this dried-up world by earthly standards.

"We took pictures of everything possible; I even tried to photograph that gigantic mural in the library, but unless Tweel's lamp was unusually rich in actinic rays, I don't suppose it'll show. And that's a pity, since it's undoubtedly the most interesting object we've found on Mars, at least from a human viewpoint.

"Tweel was a very courteous host. He took us to all the points of interest—even the new water-works."

Putz's eyes brightened at the word. "Vater-vorks?" he echoed. "For vot?"

"For the canal, naturally. They have to build up a head of water to drive it through; that's obvious." He looked at the captain. "You told me yourself that to drive water from the polar caps of Mars to the equator was equivalent to forcing it up a twenty-mile hill, because Mars is flattened at the poles and bulges at the equator just like the earth."

"That's true," agreed Harrison.

"Well," resumed Jarvis, "this city was one of the relay stations to boost the flow. Their power plant was the only one of the giant buildings that seemed to serve any useful purpose, and that was worth seeing. I wish you'd seen it, Karl; you'll have to make what you can from our pictures. It's a sun-power plant!"

Harrison and Putz stared. "Sun-power!" grunted the captain. "That's primitive!" And the engineer added an emphatic "*Ja!*" of agreement.

"Not as primitive as all that," corrected Jarvis. "The sunlight focused on a queer cylinder in the center of a big concave mirror, and they drew an electric current from it. The juice worked the pumps."

"A t'ermocouple!" ejaculated Putz.

"That sounds reasonable; you can judge by the pictures. But the power-plant had some queer things about it. The queerest was that the machinery was tended, not by Tweel's people, but by some of the barrel-shaped creatures like the ones in Xanthus!" He gazed around at the faces of his auditors; there was no comment.

"Get it?" he resumed. At their silence, he proceeded, "I see you don't. Leroy figured it out, but whether rightly or wrongly, I don't know. He thinks that the barrels and Tweel's race have a reciprocal arrangement like—well, like bees and flowers on earth. The flowers give honey for the bees; the bees carry the pollen for the flowers. See? The barrels tend the works and Tweel's people build the canal system. The Xanthus city must have been a boosting station; that explains the mysterious machines I saw. And Leroy believes further that it isn't an intelligent arrangement—not on the part of the barrels, at least—but that it's been done for so many thousands of generations that it's become instinctive—a tropism—just like the actions of ants and bees. The creatures have been bred to it!"

"Nuts!" observed Harrison. "Let's hear you explain the reason for that big empty city, then."

"Sure. Tweel's civilization is decadent, that's the reason. It's a dying race, and out of all the millions that must once have lived there, Tweel's couple of hundred companions are the remnant. They're an outpost, left to tend the source of the water at the polar cap; probably there are still a few respectable cities left somewhere on the canal system, most likely near the tropics. It's the last gasp of a race—and a race that reached a higher peak of culture than Man!"

"Huh?" said Harrison. "Then why are they dying? Lack of water?"

"I don't think so," responded the chemist. "If my guess at the city's age is right, fifteen thousand years wouldn't make enough difference in the water supply—nor a hundred thousand, for that matter. It's something else, though the water's doubtless a factor."

"*Das wasser*," cut in Putz. "Vere goes dot?"

"Even a chemist knows that!" scoffed Jarvis. "At least on earth. Here I'm not so sure, but on earth, every time there's a lightning flash, it electrolyzes some water vapor into hydrogen and oxygen, and then the hydrogen escapes into space, because terrestrial gravitation won't hold it permanently. And every time there's an earthquake, some water is lost to the interior. Slow—but damned certain." He turned to Harrison. "Right, Cap?"

"Right," conceded the captain. "But here, of course—no earthquakes, no thunderstorms—the loss must be very slow. Then why is the race dying?"

"The sun-power plant answers that," countered Jarvis. "Lack of fuel! Lack of power! No oil left, no coal left—if Mars ever had a Carboniferous Age—and no water-power—just the driblets of energy they can get from the sun. That's why they're dying."

"With the limitless energy of the atom?" exploded Harrison.

"They don't know about atomic energy. Probably never did. Must have used some other principle in their space-ship."

"Then," snapped the captain, "what makes you rate their intelligence above the human? We've finally cracked open the atom!"

"Sure we have. We had a clue, didn't we? Radium and uranium. Do you think we'd ever have learned how without those elements? We'd never even have suspected that atomic energy existed!"

"Well? Haven't they—?"

"No, they haven't. You've told me yourself that Mars has only 73 percent of the earth's density. Even a chemist can see that that means a lack of heavy metals—no osmium, no uranium, no radium. They didn't have the clue."

"Even so, that doesn't prove they're more advanced than we are. If they were *more* advanced, they'd have discovered it anyway."

"Maybe," conceded Jarvis. "I'm not claiming that we don't surpass them in some ways. But in others, they're far ahead of us."

"In what, for instance?"

"Well—socially, for one thing."

"Huh? How do you mean?"

Jarvis glanced in turn at each of the three that faced him. He hesitated. "I wonder how you chaps will take this," he muttered. "Naturally, everybody likes his own system best." He frowned. "Look here—on the earth we have three types of society, haven't we? And there's a member of each type right here. Putz lives under a dictatorship—an autocracy. Leroy's a citizen of the Sixth Commune in France. Harrison and I are Americans, members of a democracy. There you are—autocracy, democracy, communism—the three types of terrestrial societies. Tweel's people have a different system from any of us."

"Different? What is it?"

"The one no earthly nation has tried. Anarchy!"

"Anarchy!" the captain and Putz burst out together.

"That's right."

"But—" Harrison was sputtering. "What do you mean—they're ahead of us? Anarchy! Bah!"

"All right—bah!" retorted Jarvis. "I'm not saying it would work for us, or for any race of men. But it works for them."

"But—anarchy!" The captain was indignant.

"Well, when you come right down to it," argued Jarvis defensively, "anarchy is the ideal form of government, if it works. Emerson said that the best government was that which governs least, and so did Wendell Phillips, and I think George Washington. And you can't have any form of government which governs less than anarchy, which is no government at all!"

The captain was sputtering. "But—it's unnatural! Even savage tribes have their chiefs! Even a pack of wolves has its leader!"

"Well," retorted Jarvis defiantly, "that only proves that government is a primitive device, doesn't it? With a perfect race you wouldn't need it at all; government is a confession of weakness, isn't it? It's a confession that part of the people won't cooperate with the rest and that you need laws to restrain those individuals which a psychologist calls anti-social. If there were no anti-social persons—criminals and such—you wouldn't need laws or police, would you?"

"But government! You'd need government! How about public works—wars—taxes?"

"No wars on Mars, in spite of being named after the War God. No point in wars here; the population is too thin and too scattered, and besides, it takes the help of every single community to keep the canal system functioning. No taxes because, apparently, all individuals cooperate in building public works. No competition to cause trouble, because anybody can help himself to anything. As I said, with a perfect race government is entirely unnecessary."

"And do you consider the Martians a perfect race?" asked the captain grimly.

"Not at all! But they've existed so much longer than man that they're evolved, socially at least, to the point where they don't need government. They work together, that's all." Jarvis paused. "Queer, isn't it—as if Mother Nature were carrying on two experiments, one at home and one on Mars. On earth it's trial of an emotional, highly competitive race in a world of plenty; here it's the trial of a quiet, friendly race on a desert, unproductive, and inhospitable world. Everything here makes for cooperation. Why, there isn't even the factor that causes so much trouble at home—sex!"

"Huh?"

"Yeah: Tweel's people reproduce just like the barrels in the mud cities; two individuals grow a third one between them. Another proof of Leroy's theory that Martian life is neither animal nor vegetable. Besides, Tweel was a good enough host to let him poke down his beak and twiddle his feathers, and the examination convinced Leroy."

"*Oui*," confirmed the biologist. "It is true."

"But anarchy!" grumbled Harrison disgustedly. "It would show up on a dizzy, half-dead pill like Mars!"

"It'll be a good many centuries before you'll have to worry about it on earth," grinned Jarvis. He resumed his narrative.

"Well, we wandered through that sepulchral city, taking pictures of everything. And then—" Jarvis paused and shuddered—"then I took a notion to have a look at that valley we'd spotted from the rocket. I don't know why. But when we tried to steer Tweel in that direction, he set up such a squawking and screeching that I thought he'd gone batty."

"If possible!" jeered Harrison.

"So we started over there without him; he kept wailing and screaming, 'No—no—no! Tick!' but that made us the more curious. He sailed over our heads and stuck on his beak, and went through a dozen other antics, but we ploughed on, and finally he gave up and trudged disconsolately along with us.

"The valley wasn't more than a mile southeast of the city. Tweel could have covered the distance in twenty jumps, but he lagged and loitered and kept pointing back at the city and wailing 'No—no—no!' Then he'd sail up into the air and zip down on his beak directly in front of us, and we'd have to walk around him. I'd seen him do lots of crazy things before, of course; I was used to them, but it was as plain as print that he didn't want us to see that valley."

"Why?" queried Harrison.

"You asked why we came back like tramps," said Jarvis with a faint shudder. "You'll learn. We plugged along up a low rocky hill that bounded it, and as we neared the top, Tweel said, 'No breet', Tick! No breet'!' Well, those were the words he used to describe the silicon monster; they were also the words he had used to tell me that the image of Fancy Long, the one that had almost lured me to the dream-beast, wasn't real. I remembered that, but it meant nothing to me—then!

"Right after that, Tweel said, 'You one-one-two, he one-one-two,' and then I began to see. That was the phrase he had used to explain the dream-beast to tell me that what I thought, the creature thought—to tell me how the thing lured its victims by their own desires. So I warned Leroy; it seemed to me that even the dream-beast couldn't be dangerous if we were warned and expecting it. Well, I was wrong!

"As we reached the crest, Tweel spun his head completely around, so his feet were forward but his eyes looked backward, as if he feared to gaze into the valley. Leroy and I stared out over it, just a gray waste like this around us, with the gleam of the south polar cap far beyond its southern rim. That's what it was one second; the next it was—Paradise!"

"What?" exclaimed the captain.

Jarvis turned to Leroy. "Can you describe it?" he asked.

The biologist waved helpless hands, "C'est impossible!" he whispered. "Il me rend muet!"

"It strikes me dumb, too," muttered Jarvis. "I don't know how to tell it; I'm a chemist, not a poet. Paradise is as good a word as I can think of, and that's not at all right. It was Paradise and Hell in one!"

"Will you talk sense?" growled Harrison.

"As much of it as makes sense. I tell you, one moment we were looking at a grey valley covered with blobby plants, and the next—Lord! You can't imagine that next moment! How would you like to see all your dreams made real? Every desire you'd ever had gratified? Everything you'd ever wanted there for the taking?"

"I'd like it fine!" said the captain.

"You're welcome, then!—not only your noble desires, remember! Every good impulse, yes—but also every nasty little wish, every vicious thought, everything you'd ever desired, good or bad! The dream-beasts are marvelous salesmen, but they lack the moral sense!"

"The dream-beasts?"

"Yes. It was a valley of them. Hundreds, I suppose, maybe thousands. Enough, at any rate, to spread out a complete picture of your desires, even all the forgotten ones that must have been drawn out of the subconscious. A Paradise—of sorts! I saw a dozen Fancy Longs, in every costume I'd ever admired on her, and some I must have imagined. I saw every beautiful woman I've ever known, and all of them pleading for my attention. I saw every lovely place I'd ever wanted to be, all packed queerly into that little valley. And I saw—other things." He shook his head soberly. "It wasn't all exactly pretty. Lord! How much of the beast is left in us! I suppose if every man alive could have one look at that weird valley, and could see just once what nastiness is hidden in him—well, the world might gain by it. I thanked heaven afterwards that Leroy—and even Tweel—saw their own pictures and not mine!"

Jarvis paused again, then resumed, "I turned dizzy with a sort of ecstasy. I closed my eyes—and with eyes closed, I still saw the whole thing! That beautiful, evil, devilish panorama was in my mind, not my eyes. That's how those fiends work—through the mind. I knew it was the dream-beasts; I didn't need Tweel's wail of 'No breet'! No breet'!' But—*I couldn't keep away!* I knew it was death beckoning, but it was worth it for one moment with the vision."

"Which particular vision?" asked Harrison dryly.

Jarvis flushed. "No matter," he said. "But beside me I heard Leroy's cry of 'Yvonne! Yvonne!' and I knew he was trapped like myself. I fought for sanity; I kept telling myself to stop, and all the time I was rushing headlong into the snare!

"Then something tripped me. Tweel! He had come leaping from behind; as I crashed down I saw him flash over me straight toward—toward what I'd been running to, with his vicious beak pointed right at her heart!"

"Oh!" nodded the captain. "*Her* heart!"

"Never mind that. When I scrambled up, that particular image was gone, and Tweel was in a twist of black ropey arms, just as when I first saw him. He'd missed a vital point in the beast's anatomy, but was jabbing away desperately with his beak.

"Somehow, the spell had lifted, or partially lifted. I wasn't five feet from Tweel, and it took a terrific struggle, but I managed to raise my revolver and put a Boland shell into the beast. Out came a spurt of horrible black corruption, drenching Tweel and me—and I guess the sickening smell of it helped to destroy the illusion of that valley of beauty. Anyway, we managed to get Leroy away from the devil that had him, and the three of us staggered to the ridge and over. I had presence of mind enough to raise my camera over the crest and take a shot of the valley, but I'll bet it shows nothing but gray waste and writhing horrors. What we saw was with our minds, not our eyes."

Jarvis paused and shuddered. "The brute half poisoned Leroy," he continued. "We dragged ourselves back to the auxiliary, called you, and did what we could to treat ourselves. Leroy took a long dose of the cognac that we had with us; we didn't dare try anything of Tweel's because his metabolism is so different from ours that what cured him might kill us. But the cognac seemed to work, and so, after I'd done one other thing I wanted to do, we came back here—and that's all."

"All, is it?" queried Harrison. "So you've solved all the mysteries of Mars, eh?"

"Not by a damned sight!" retorted Jarvis. "Plenty of unanswered questions are left."

"*Ja!*" snapped Putz. "Der evaporation—dot iss shtopped how?"

"In the canals? I wondered about that, too; in those thousands of miles, and against this low air-pressure, you'd think they'd lose a lot. But the answer's simple; they float a skin of oil on the water."

Putz nodded, but Harrison cut in. "Here's a puzzler. With only coal and oil—just combustion or electric power—where'd they get the energy to build a planet-wide canal system, thousands and thousands of miles of 'em? Think of the job we had cutting the Panama Canal to sea level, and then answer that!"

"Easy!" grinned Jarvis. "Martian gravity and Martian air—that's the answer. Figure it out: First, the dirt they dug only weighed a third its earth-weight. Second, a steam engine here expands against ten pounds per square inch less air pressure than on earth. Third, they could build the engine three times as large here with no greater internal weight. And fourth, the whole planet's nearly level. Right, Putz?"

The engineer nodded. "*Ja!* Der shteam—engine—it iss *sieben-und zwanzig*—twenty-seven times so effective here."

"Well, there *does* go the last mystery then," mused Harrison.

"Yeah?" queried Jarvis sardonically. "You answer these, then. What was the nature of that vast empty city? Why do the Martians *need* canals, since we never saw them eat or drink? Did they really visit the earth before the dawn of history, and, if not atomic energy, what powered their ship? Since Tweel's race seems to need little or no water, are they merely operating the canals for some higher creature that does? *Are* there other intelligences on Mars? If not, what was the demon-faced imp we saw with the book? There are a few mysteries for you!"

"I know one or two more!" growled Harrison, glaring suddenly at little Leroy. "You and your visions! 'Yvonne!' eh? Your wife's name is Marie, isn't it?"

The little biologist turned crimson. "*Oui*," he admitted unhappily. He turned pleading eyes on the captain. "Please," he said. "In Paris *tout le monde*—everybody he think differently of those things—no?" He twisted uncomfortably. "Please, you will not tell Marie, *n'est-ce pas?*"

Harrison chuckled. "None of my business," he said. "One more question, Jarvis. What was the one other thing you did before returning here?"

Jarvis looked diffident. "Oh—that." He hesitated. "Well I sort of felt we owed Tweel a lot, so after some trouble, we coaxed him into the rocket and sailed him out to the wreck of the first one, over on Thyle II. Then," he finished apologetically, "I showed him the atomic blast, got it working—and gave it to him!"

"You *what?*" roared the Captain. "You turned something as powerful as that over to an alien race—maybe some day as an enemy race?"

"Yes, I did," said Jarvis. "Look here," he argued defensively. "This lousy, dried-up pill of a desert called Mars'll never support much human population. The Sahara desert is just as good a field for imperialism, and a lot closer to home. So we'll never find Tweel's race enemies. The only value we'll find here is commercial trade with the Martians. Then why shouldn't I give Tweel a chance for survival? With atomic energy, they can run their canal system a hundred per cent instead of only one out of five, as Putz's observations showed. They can repopulate those ghostly cities; they can resume their arts and industries; they can trade with the nations of the earth—and I'll bet they can teach us a few things," he paused, "if they can figure out the atomic blast, and I'll lay odds they can. They're no fools, Tweel and his ostrich-faced Martians!"